HANSEL AND GRETEL

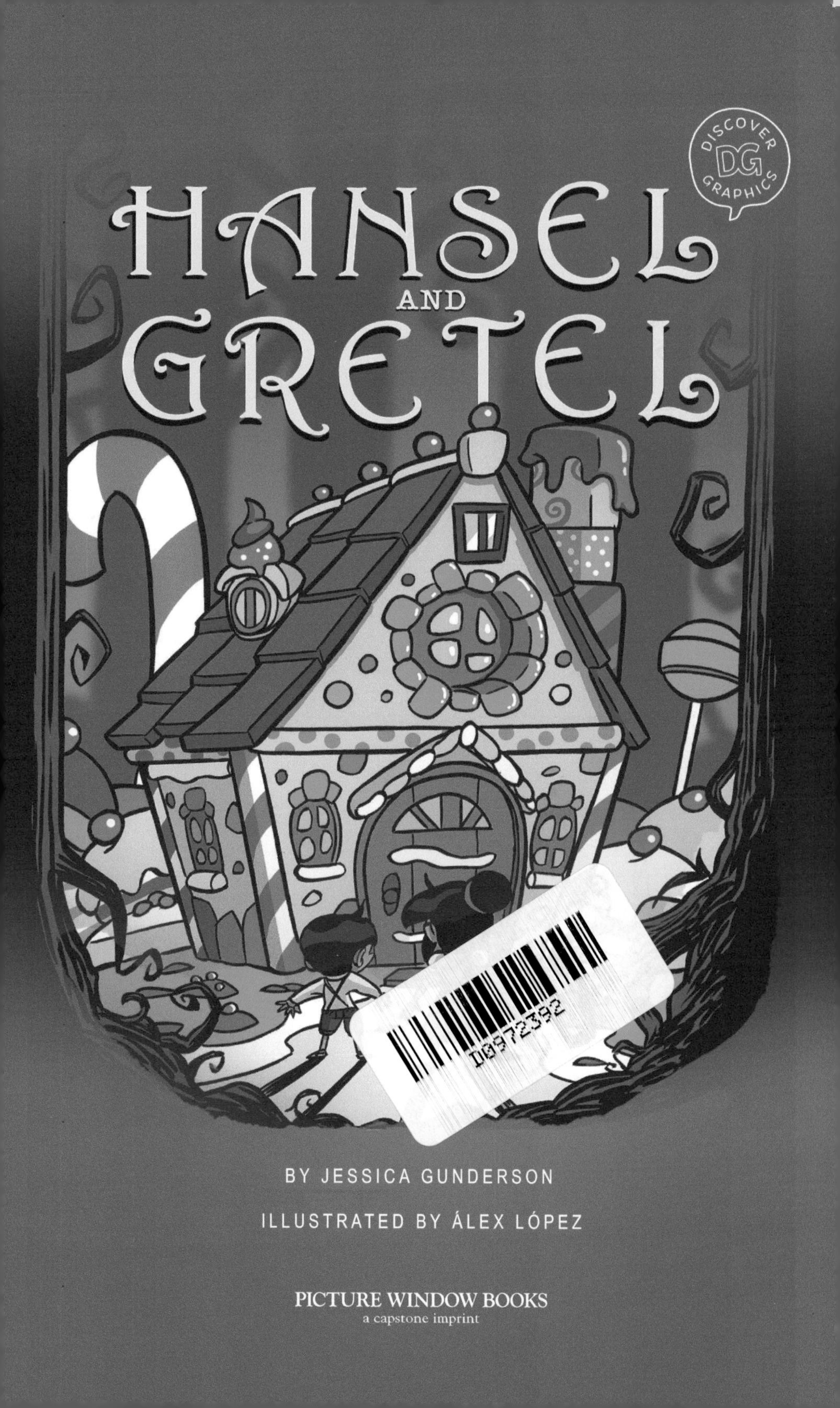

BY JESSICA GUNDERSON

ILLUSTRATED BY ÁLEX LÓPEZ

PICTURE WINDOW BOOKS
a capstone imprint

Discover Graphics is published by Picture Window Books,
an imprint of Capstone.
1710 Roe Crest Drive
North Mankato, Minnesota 56003
www.capstonepub.com

Library of Congress Cataloging-in-Publication Data is available on the Library of Congress website.
ISBN: 978-1-5158-7120-0 (library binding)
ISBN: 978-1-5158-7273-3 (paperback)
ISBN: 978-1-5158-7127-9 (ebook PDF)

Summary: Revisit the tale of Hansel and Gretel. Left in the woods, the two encounter a witch. Will the brother and sister find their way out of the forest safely, or be left at the hands of the witch?

Editorial Credits
Editor: Mari Bolte; Designer: Kay Fraser; Media Researcher: Tracy Cummins; Production Specialist: Katy LaVigne

WORDS TO KNOW

gingerbread—a cake or cookie made with molasses and flavored with ginger

skittles—an outdoor game similar to bowling; nine wooden pins called skittles are knocked down with a wooden disc or ball

plump—somewhat fat or round

woodcutter—a person who who chops wood for a living

Printed in the United States 4913

CAST OF CHARACTERS

Hansel and **Gretel** live with their father and stepmother at the edge of the woods. They are clever children.

Douglas is Hansel and Gretel's father. He is a woodcutter. He loves his children but is scared of his wife.

Hansel and Gretel's stepmother, **Hornbeam**, doesn't like her stepchildren and wants to get rid of them.

Skittle the Witch lives in a cottage deep in the woods. Her home is made of candy. But she has a dark secret.

HOW TO READ A GRAPHIC NOVEL

Graphic novels are easy to read. Boxes called panels show you how to follow the story. Look at the panels from left to right and top to bottom.

Read the word boxes and word balloons from left to right as well. Don't forget the sound and action words in the pictures.

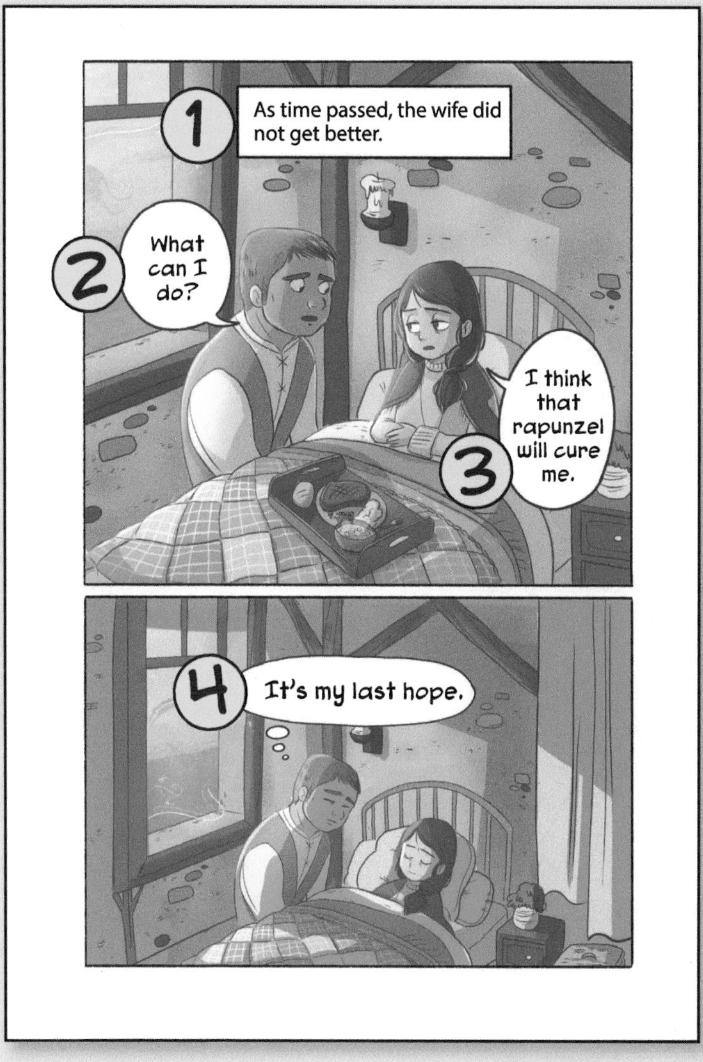
1
As time passed, the wife did not get better.
2
What can I do?
I think that rapunzel will cure me.
3
4
It's my last hope.

The pictures and the words work together to tell the whole story.

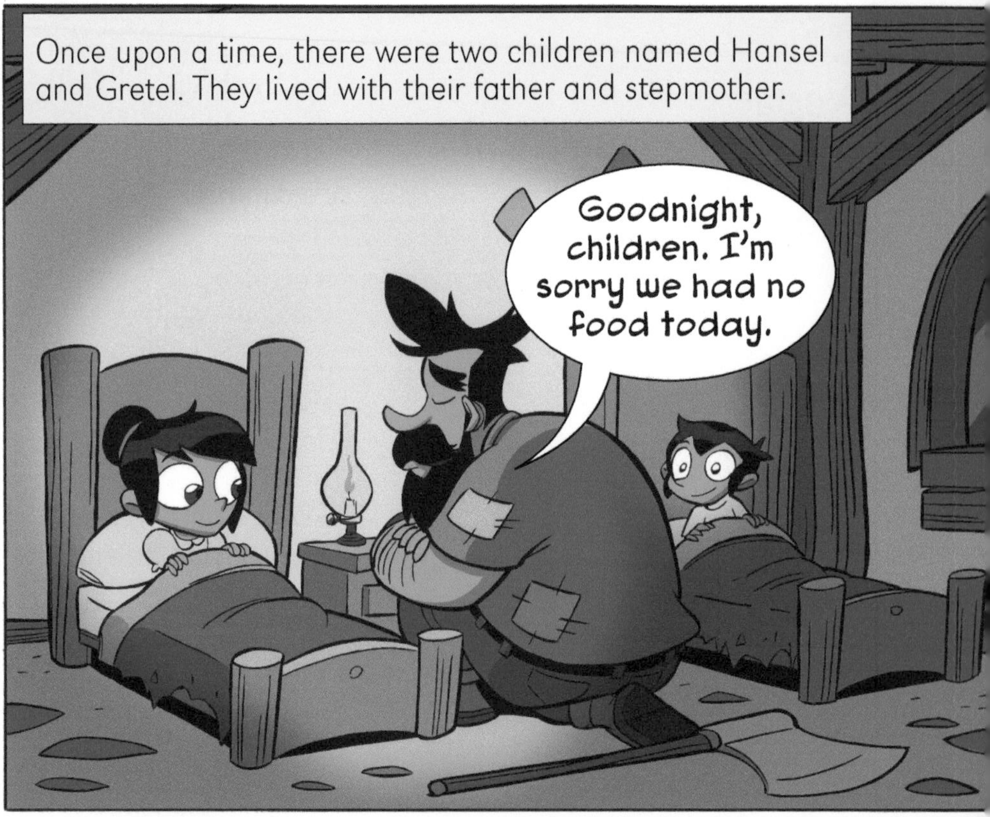

Once upon a time, there were two children named Hansel and Gretel. They lived with their father and stepmother.
Goodnight, children. I'm sorry we had no food today.

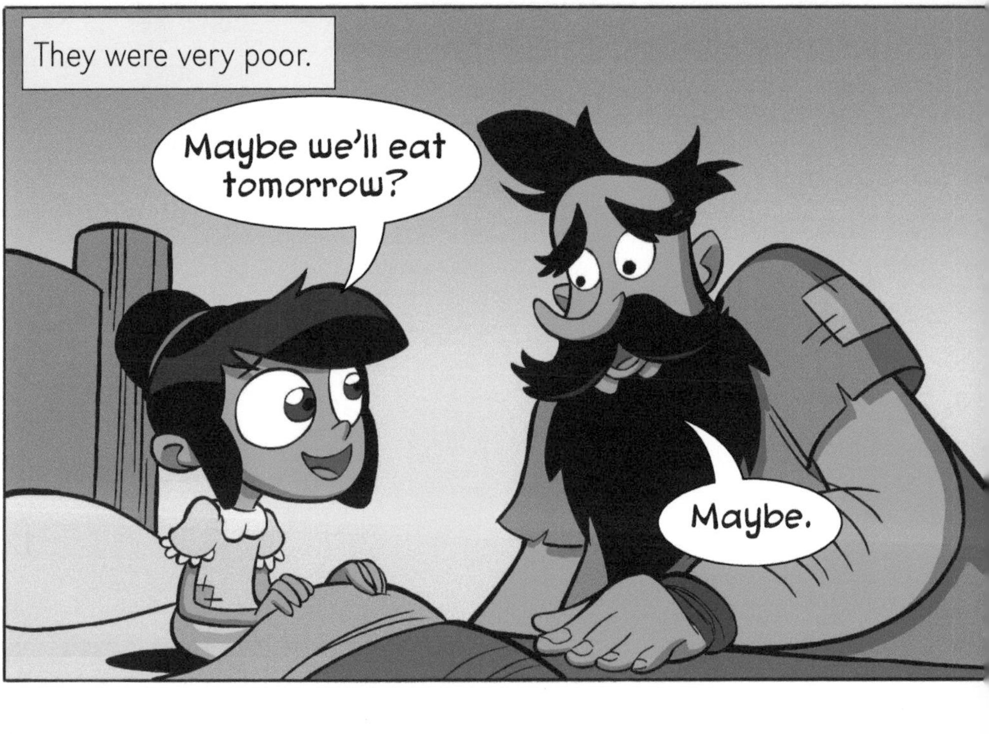

They were very poor.
Maybe we'll eat tomorrow?
Maybe.

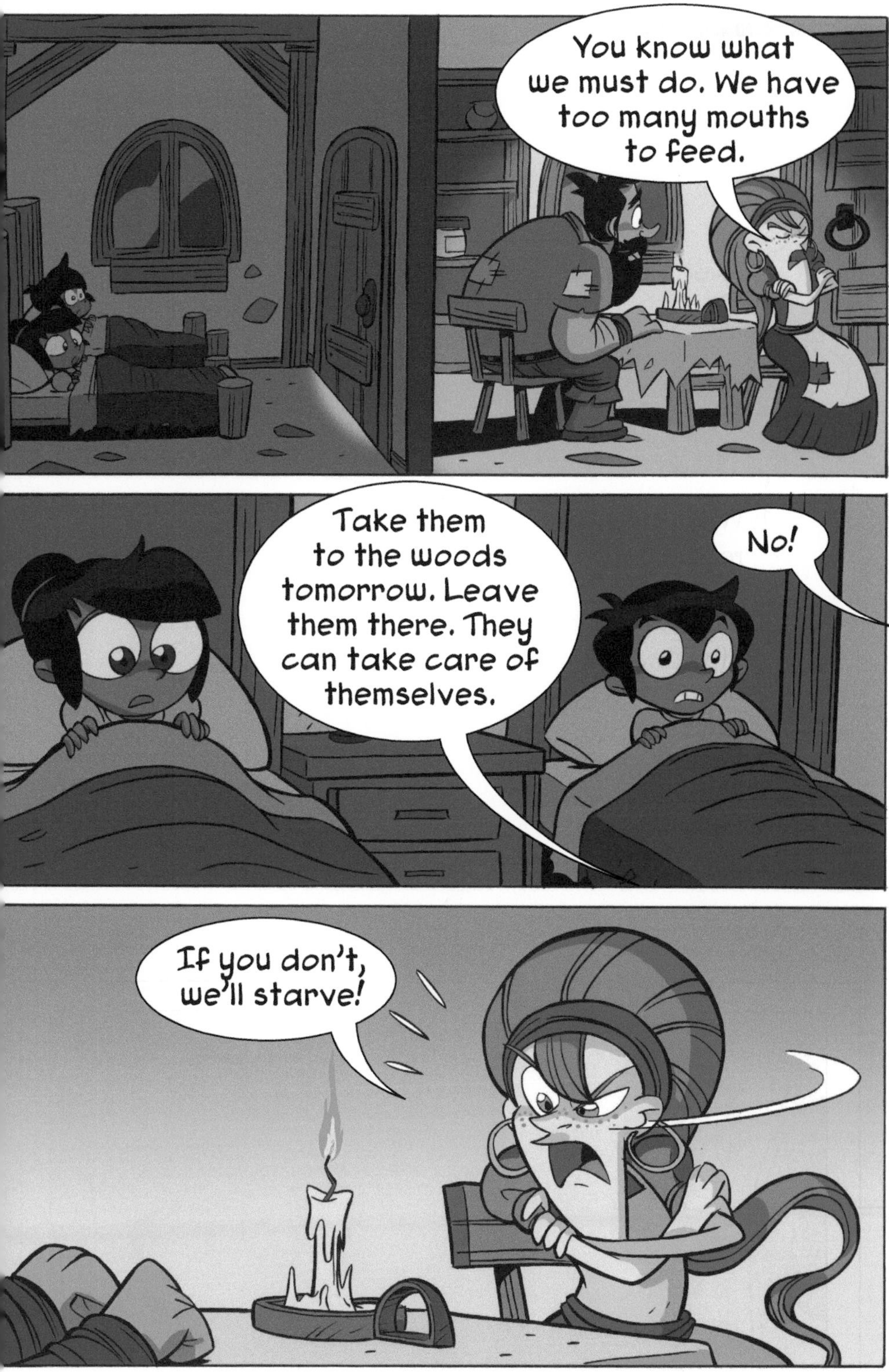
You know what we must do. We have too many mouths to feed.
Take them to the woods tomorrow. Leave them there. They can take care of themselves.
No!
If you don't, we'll starve!

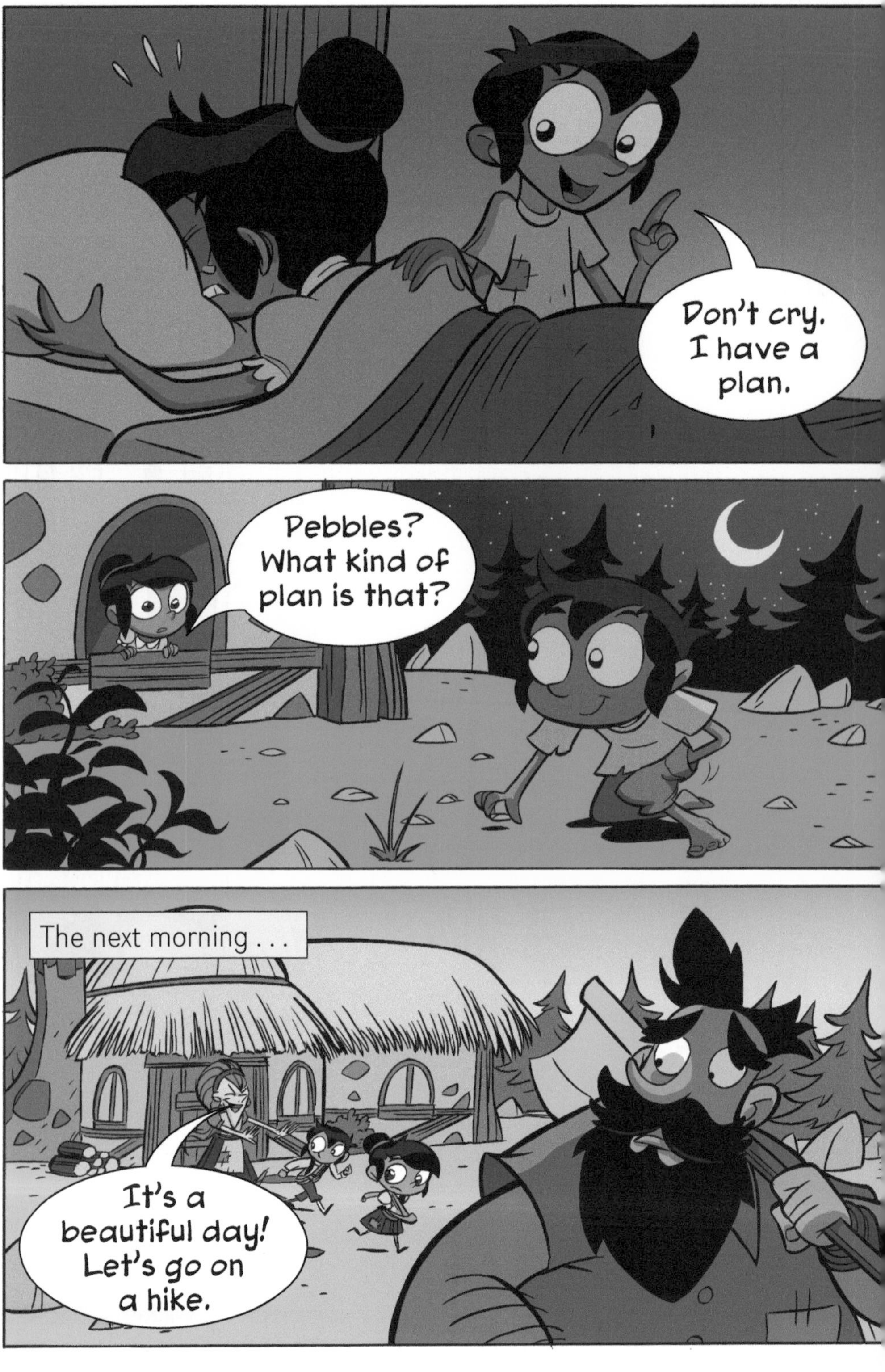
Don't cry.
I have a
plan.
Pebbles?
What kind of
plan is that?
The next morning . . .
It's a
beautiful day!
Let's go on
a hike.

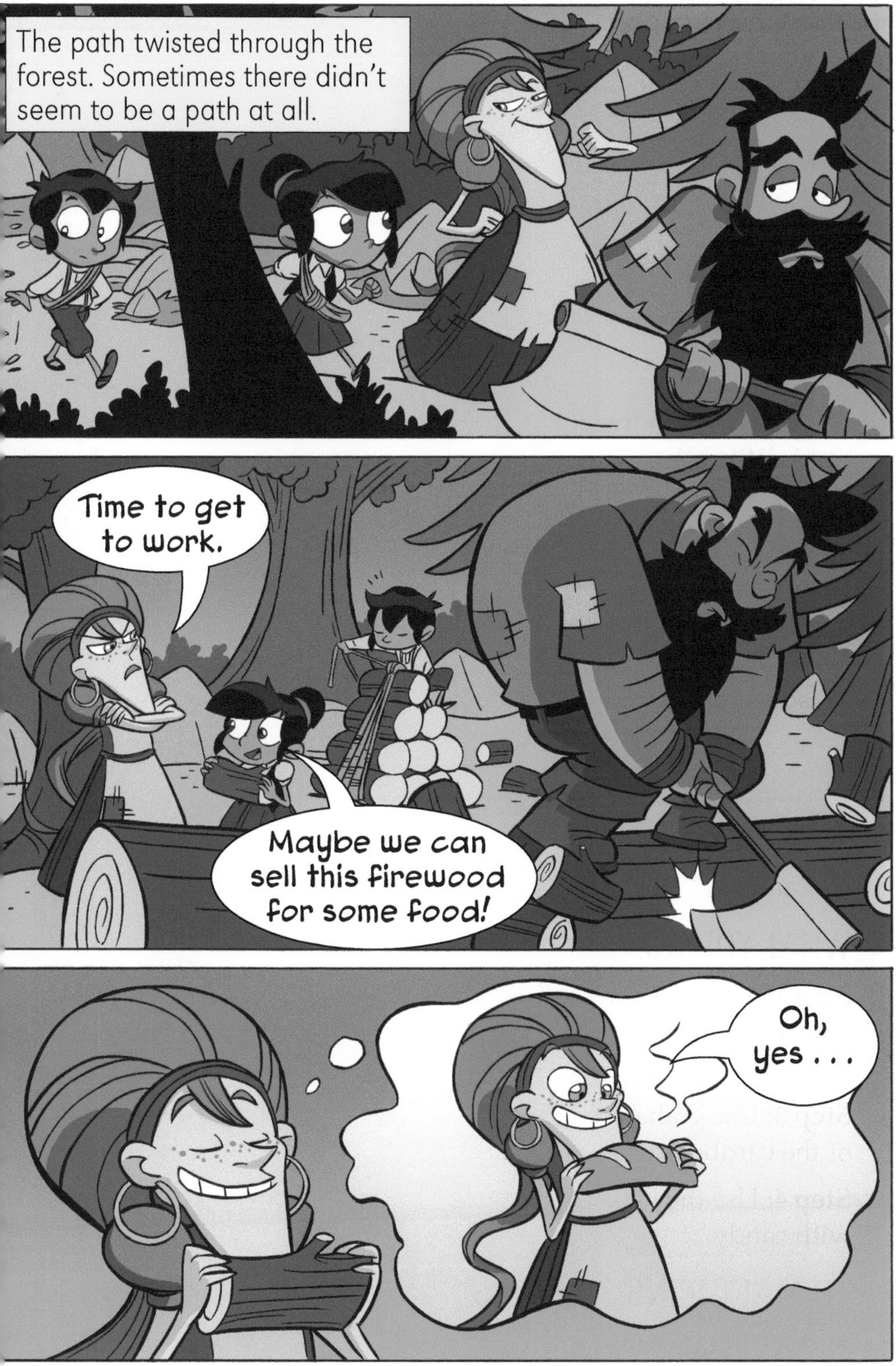
The path twisted through the forest. Sometimes there didn't seem to be a path at all.
Time to get to work.
Maybe we can sell this firewood for some food!
Oh, yes . . .

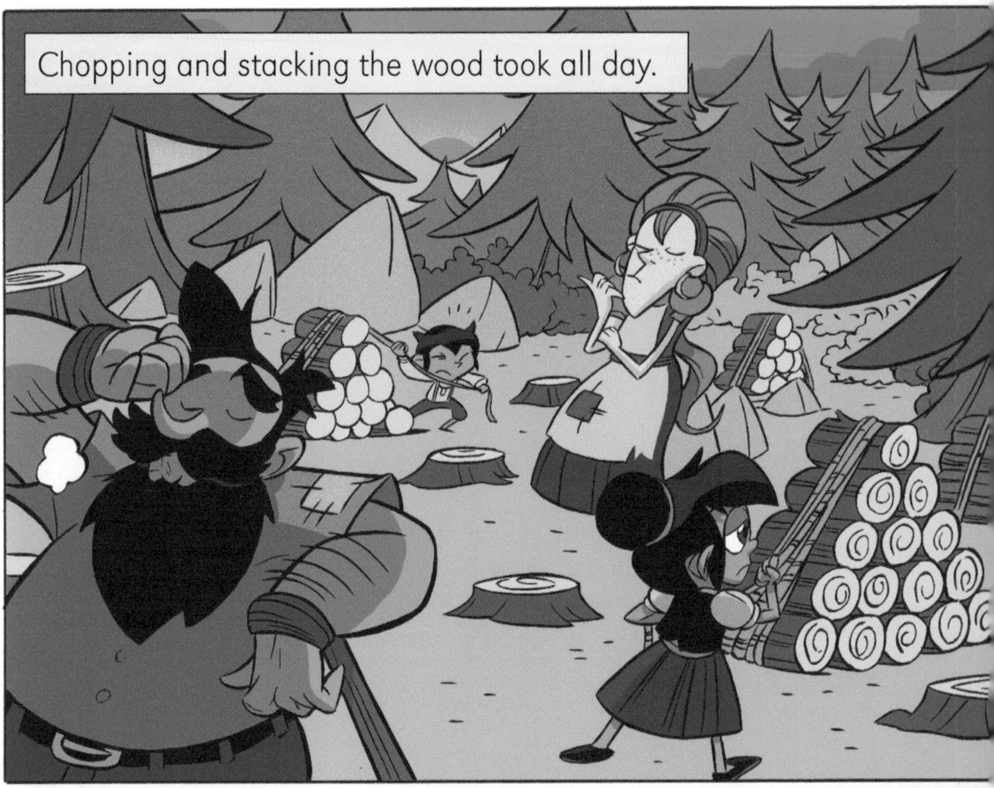
Chopping and stacking the wood took all day.

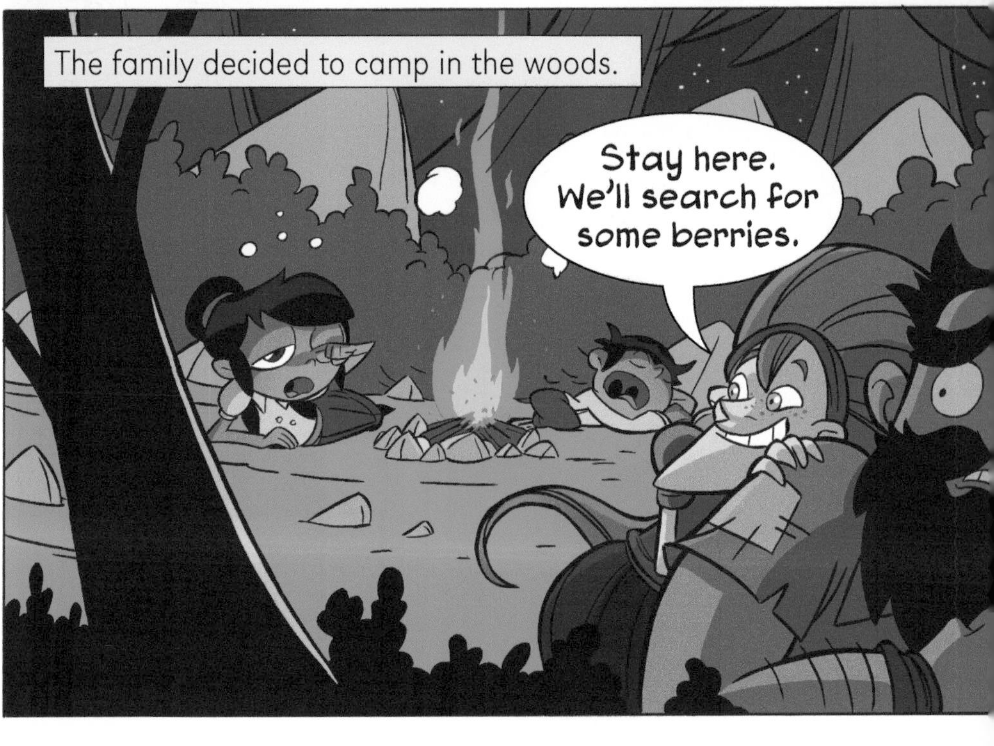
The family decided to camp in the woods.
Stay here. We'll search for some berries.

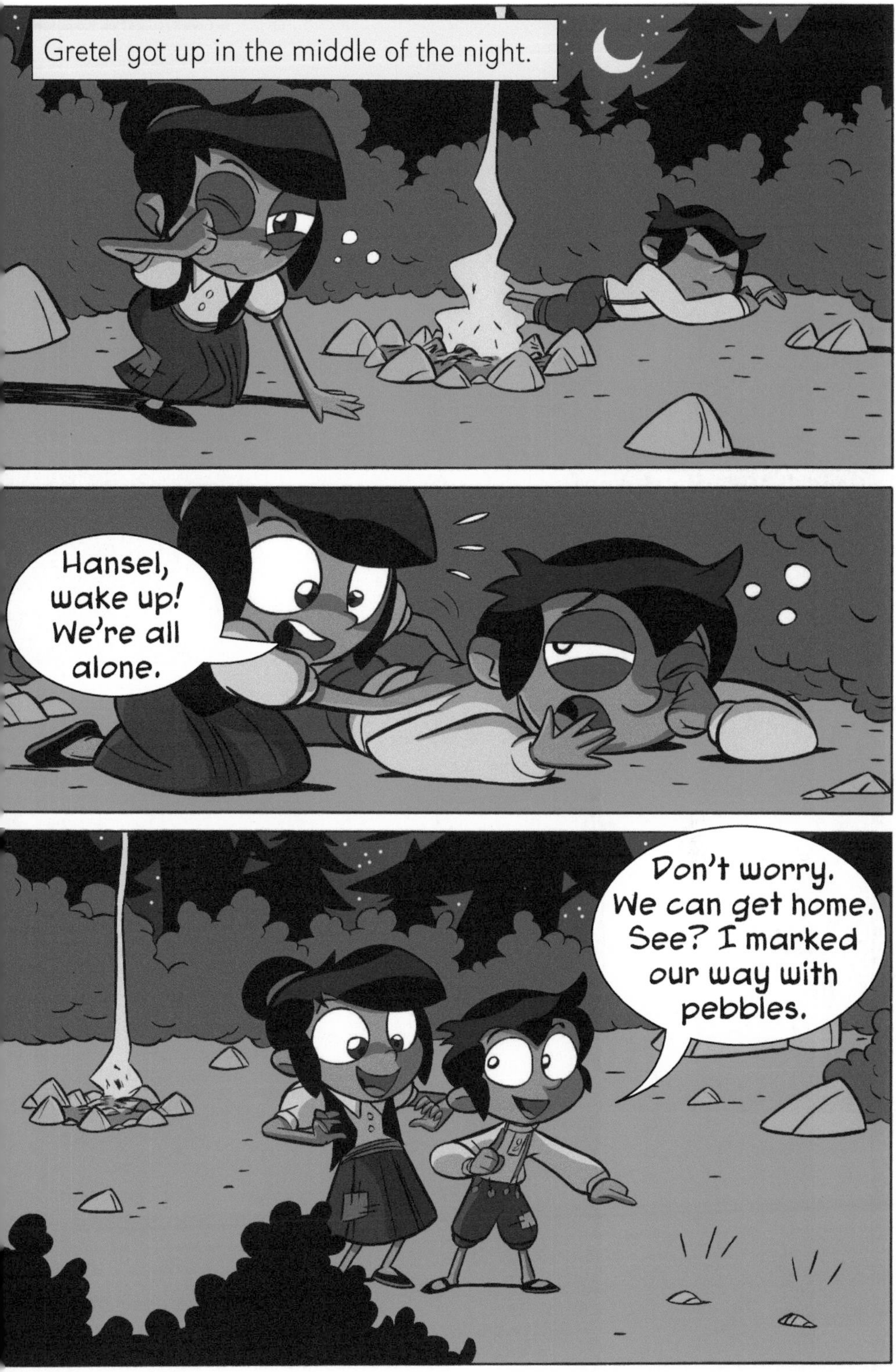

Gretel got up in the middle of the night.
Hansel, wake up! We're all alone.
Don't worry. We can get home. See? I marked our way with pebbles.

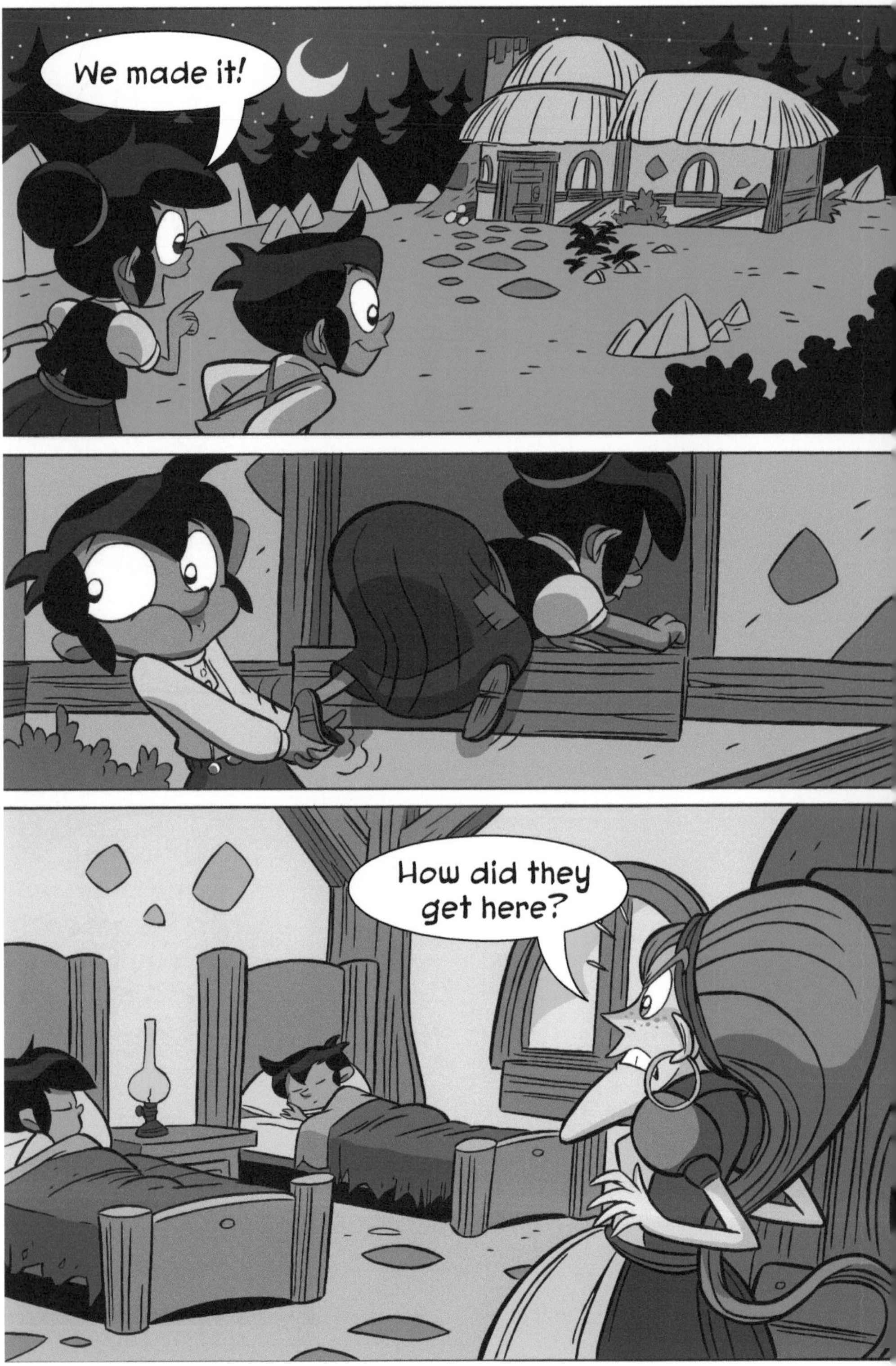
We made it!
How did they get here?

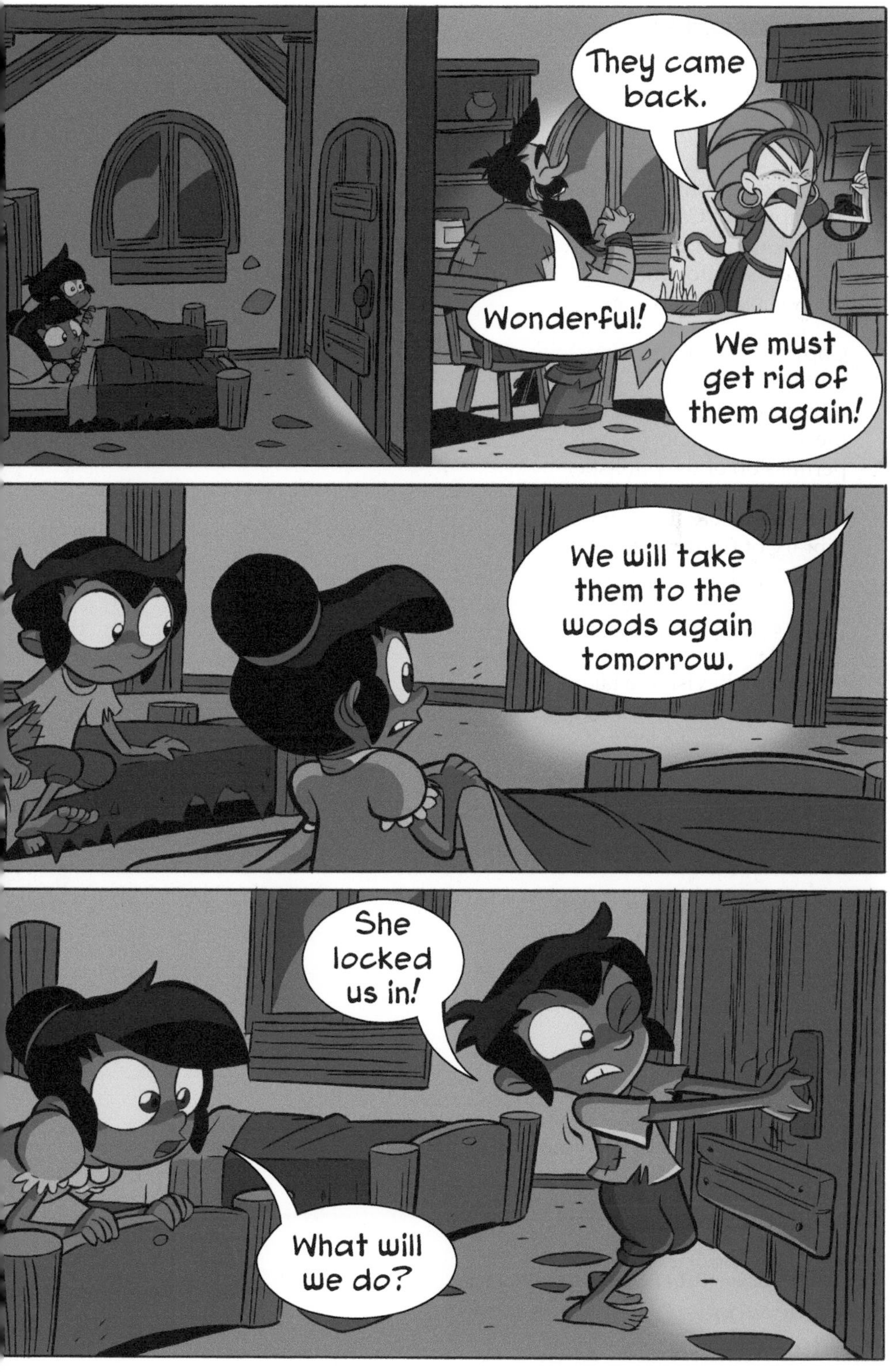
They came back.
Wonderful!
We must get rid of them again!
We will take them to the woods again tomorrow.
She locked us in!
What will we do?

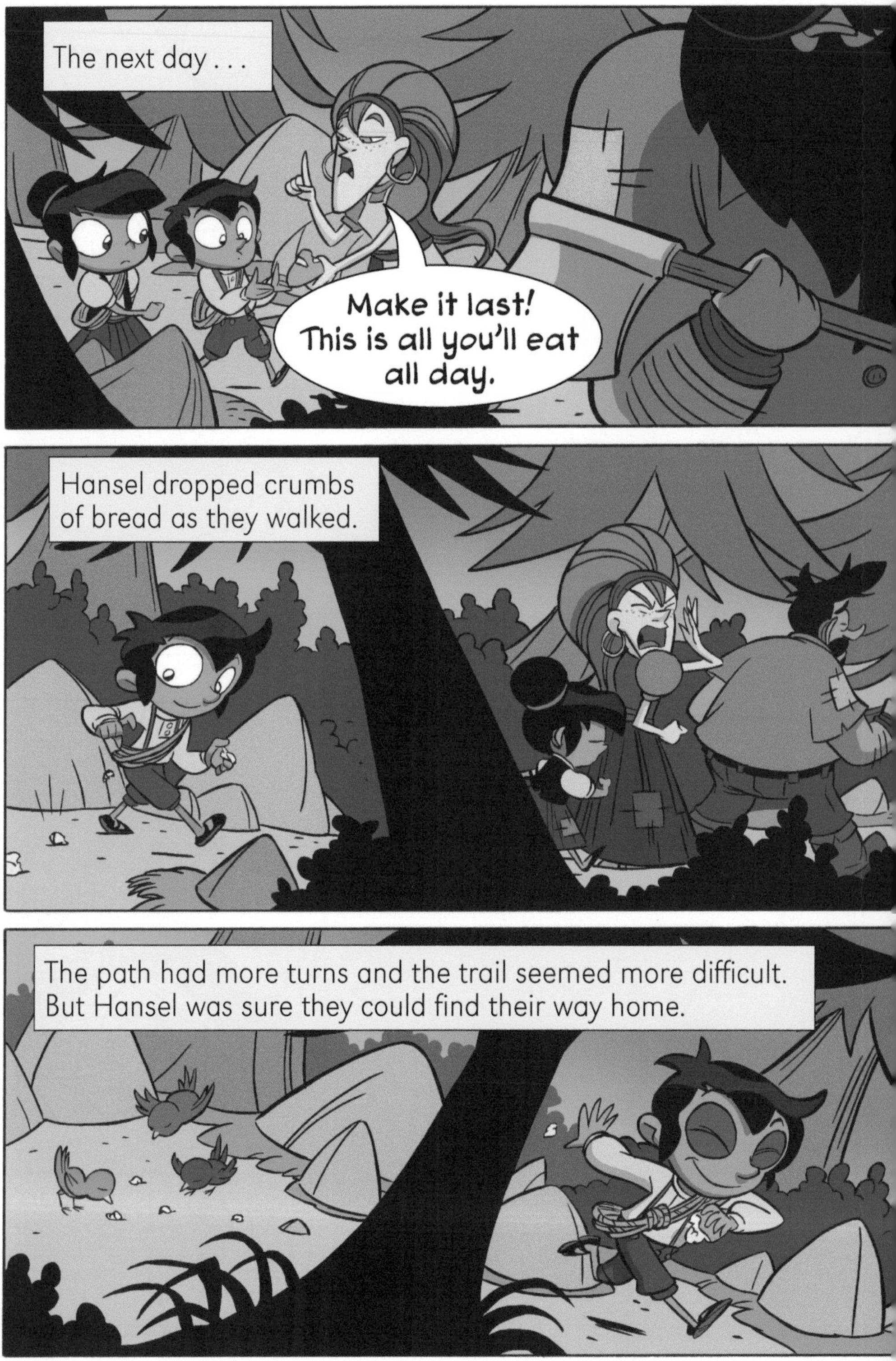

The next day . . .
Make it last! This is all you'll eat all day.
Hansel dropped crumbs of bread as they walked.
The path had more turns and the trail seemed more difficult. But Hansel was sure they could find their way home.

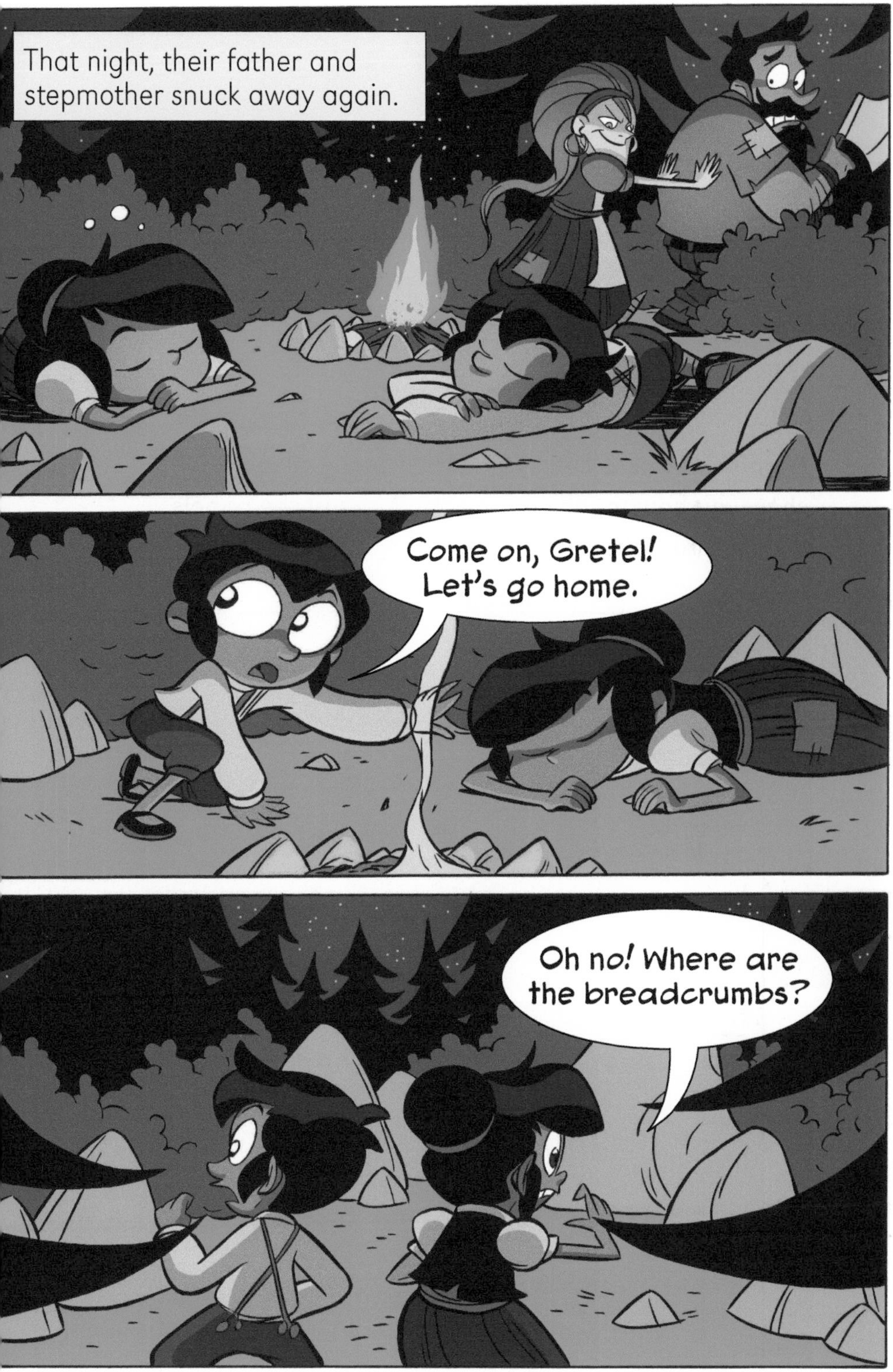
That night, their father and stepmother snuck away again.
Come on, Gretel! Let's go home.
Oh no! Where are the breadcrumbs?

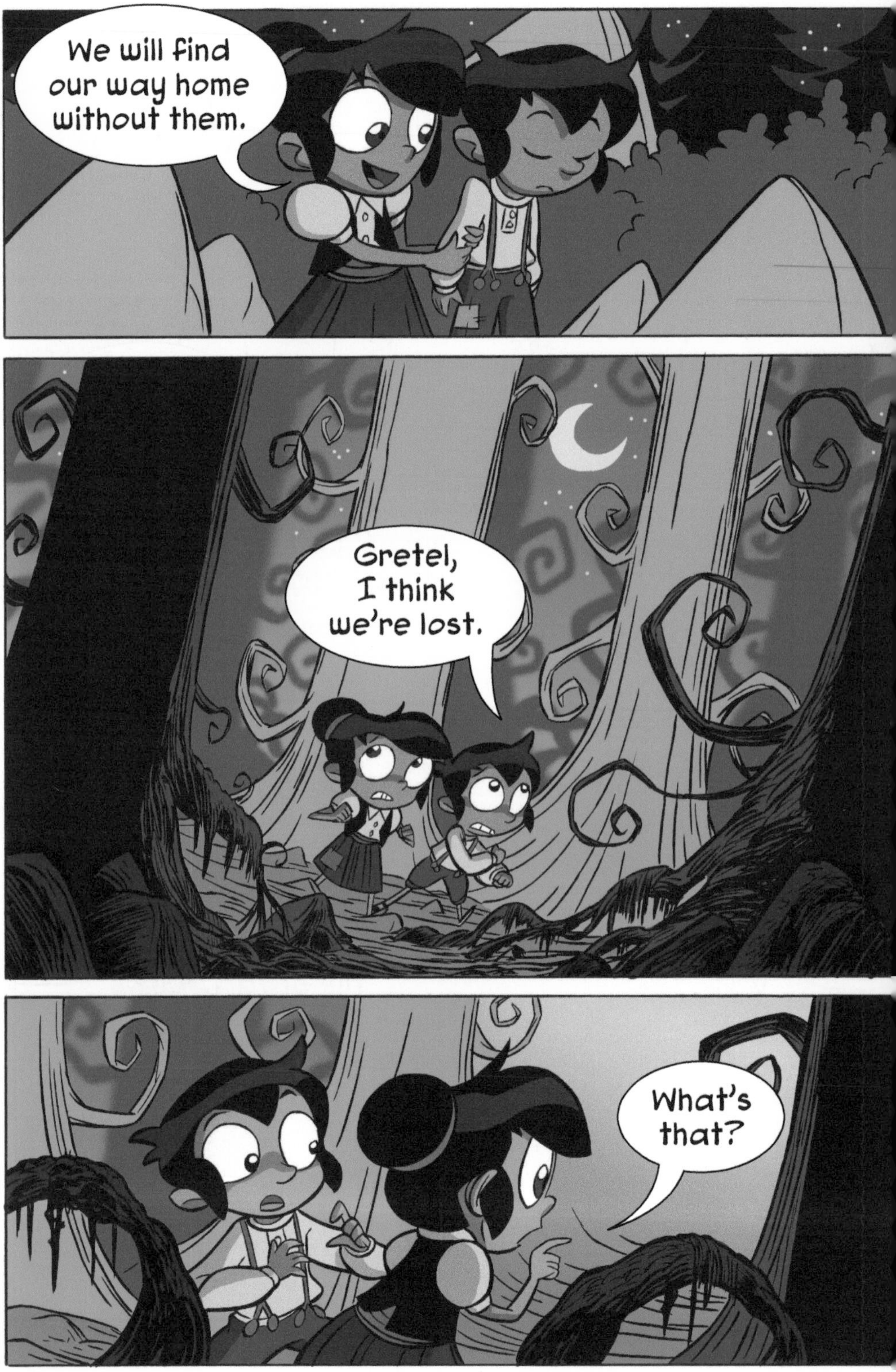
We will find our way home without them.
Gretel, I think we're lost.
What's that?

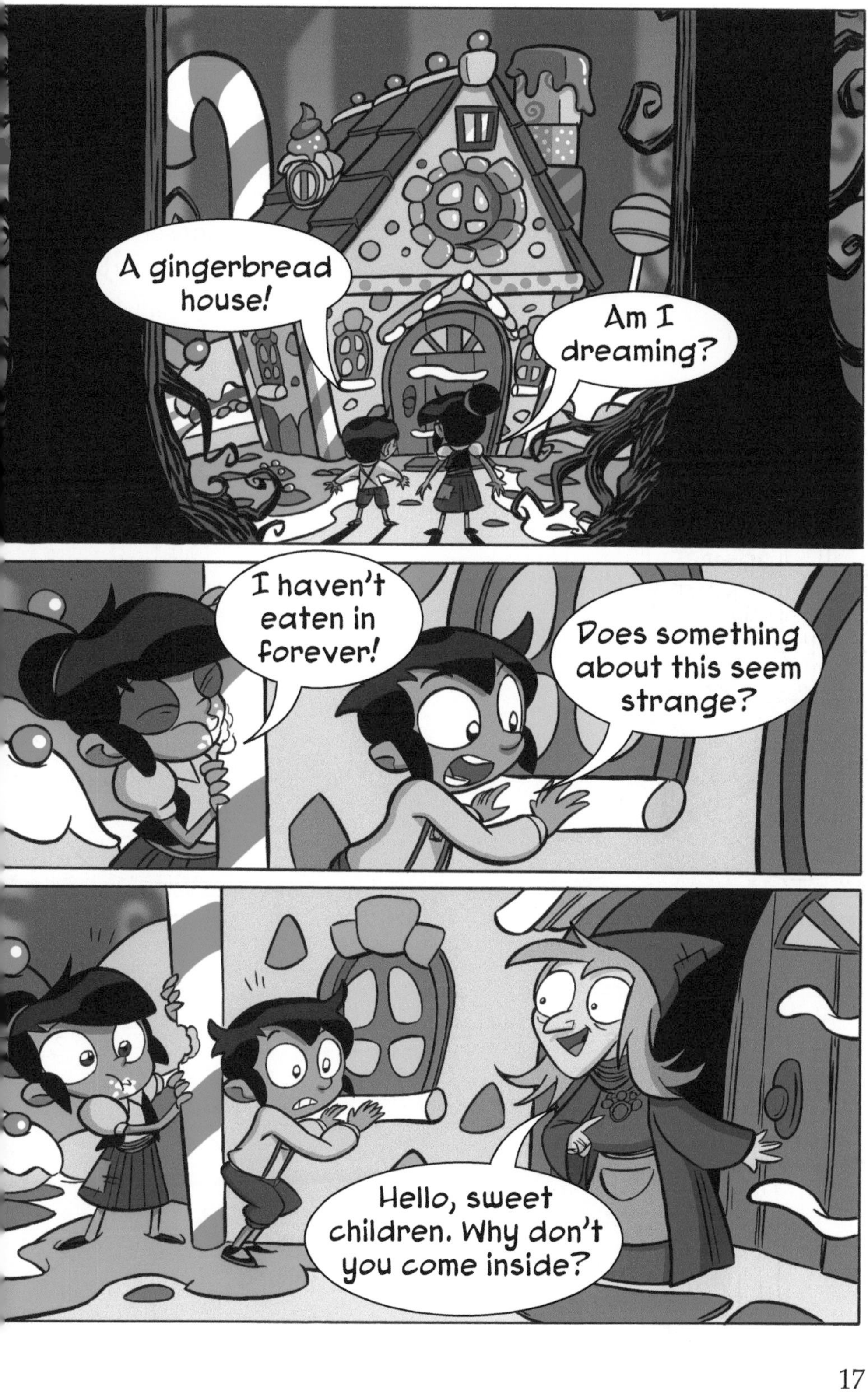
A gingerbread house!
Am I dreaming?
I haven't eaten in forever!
Does something about this seem strange?
Hello, sweet children. Why don't you come inside?

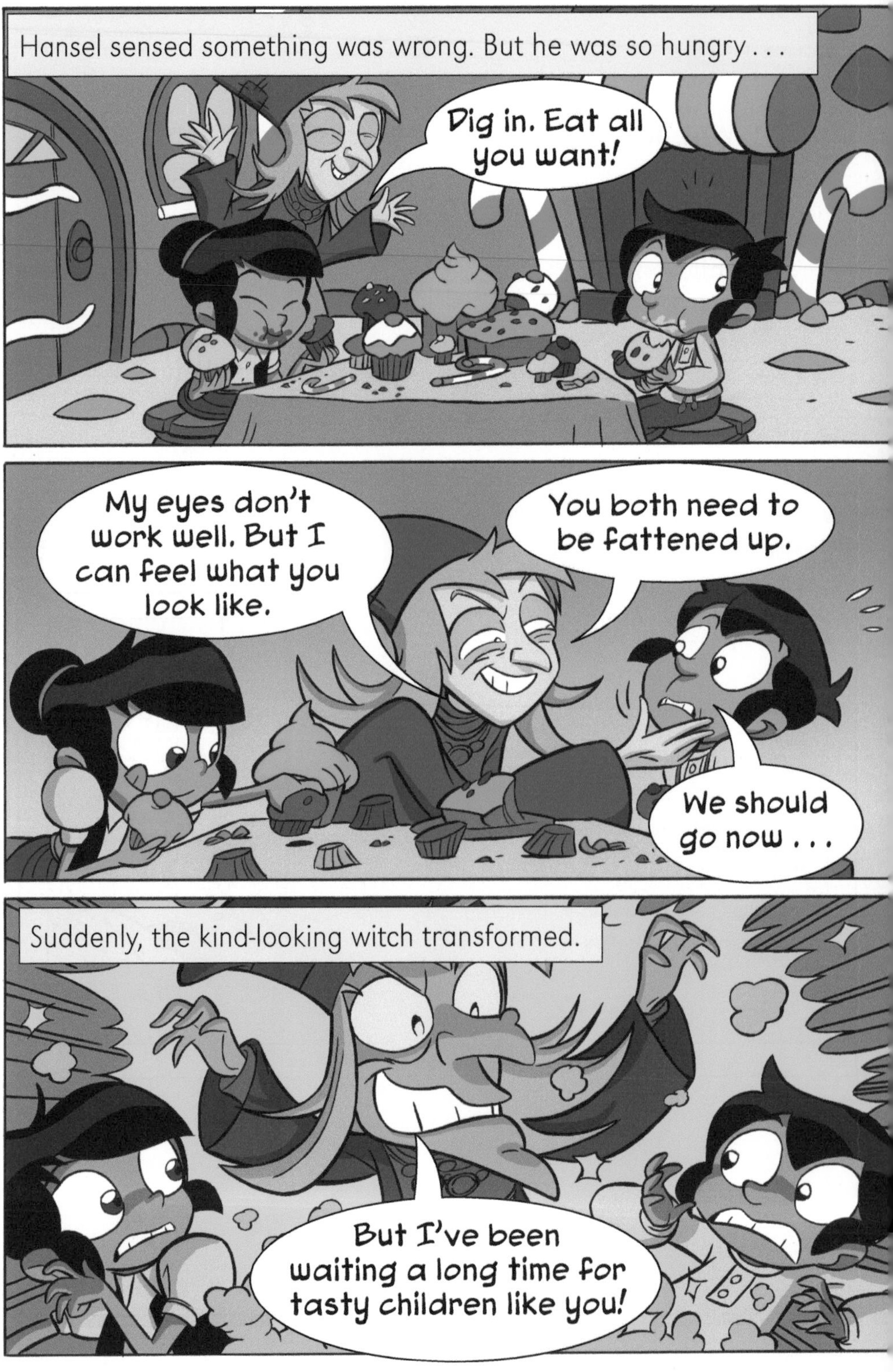
Hansel sensed something was wrong. But he was so hungry . . .
Dig in. Eat all you want!
My eyes don't work well. But I can feel what you look like.
You both need to be fattened up.
We should go now . . .
Suddenly, the kind-looking witch transformed.
But I've been waiting a long time for tasty children like you!

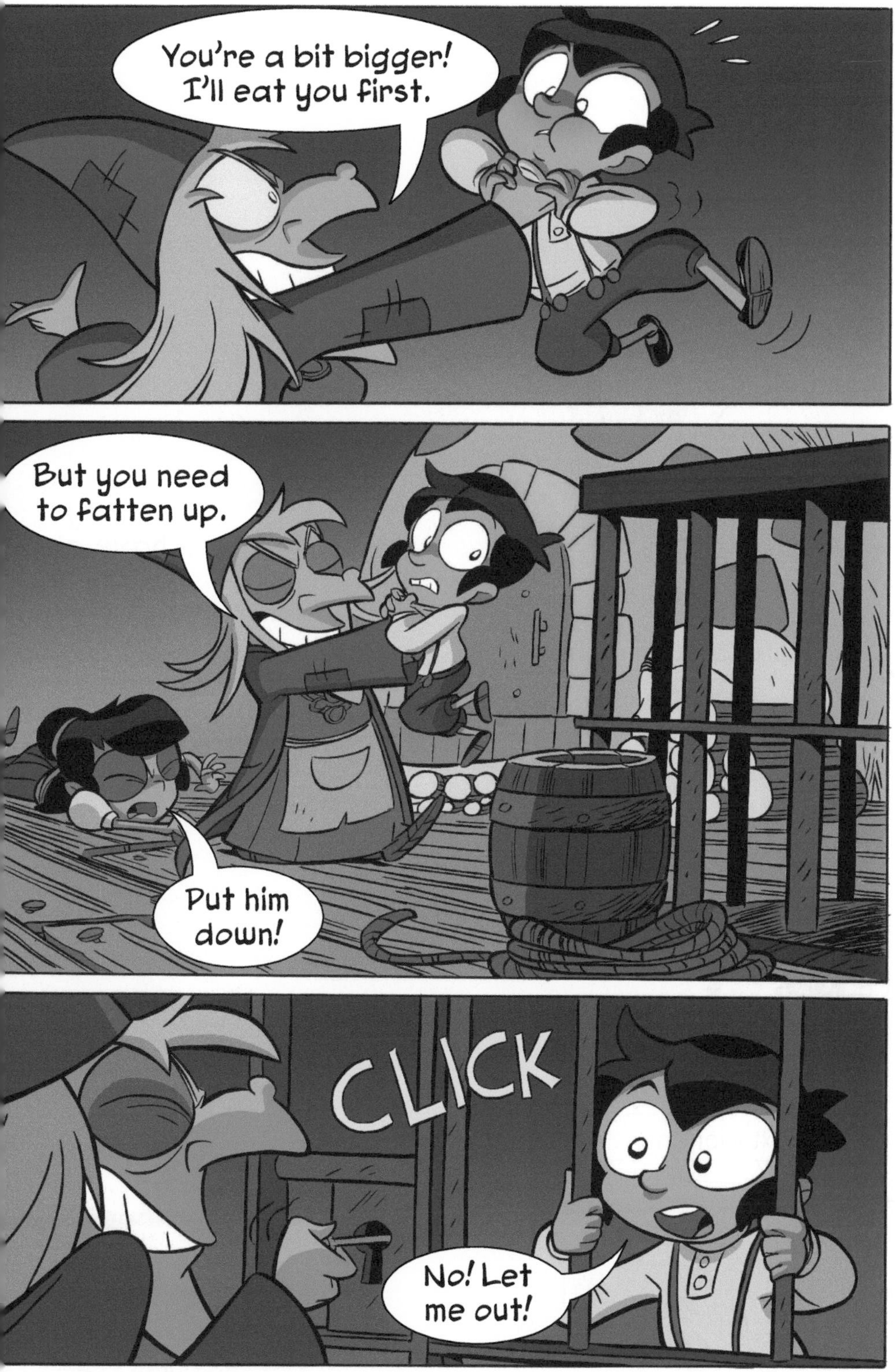
You're a bit bigger! I'll eat you first.
But you need to fatten up.
Put him down!
CLICK
No! Let me out!

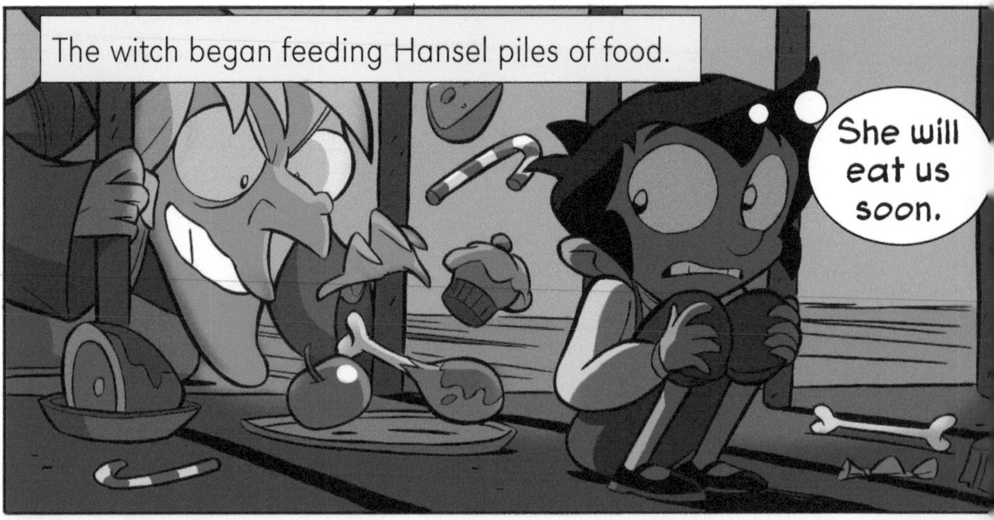
The witch began feeding Hansel piles of food.
She will eat us soon.

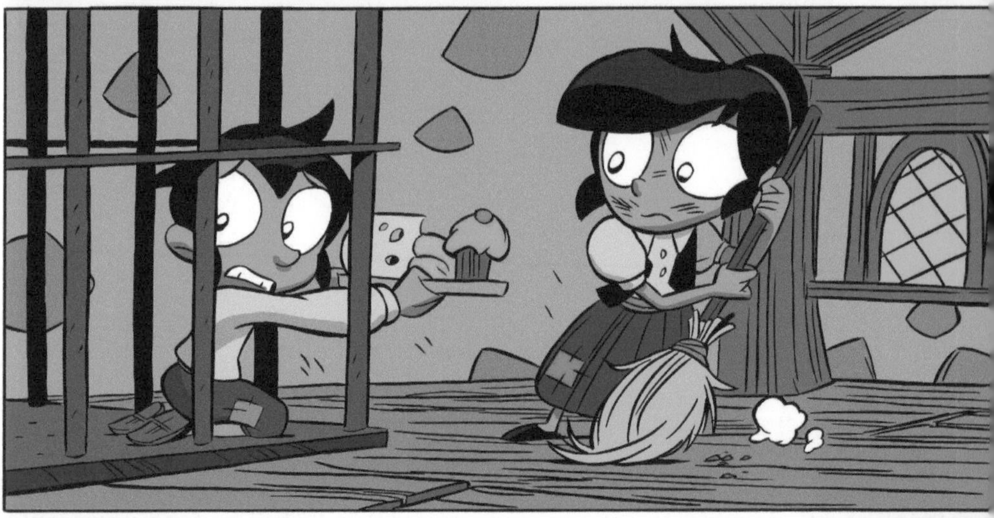

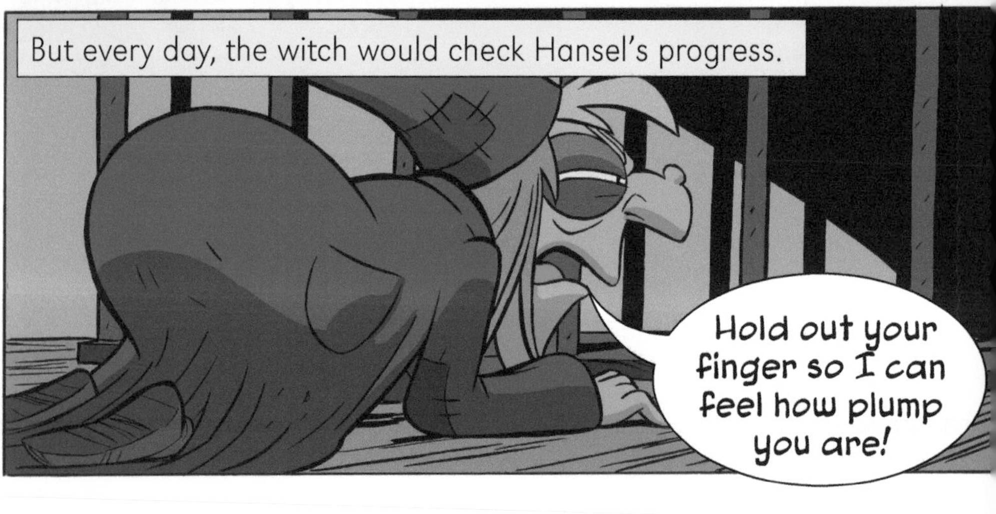
But every day, the witch would check Hansel's progress.
Hold out your finger so I can feel how plump you are!

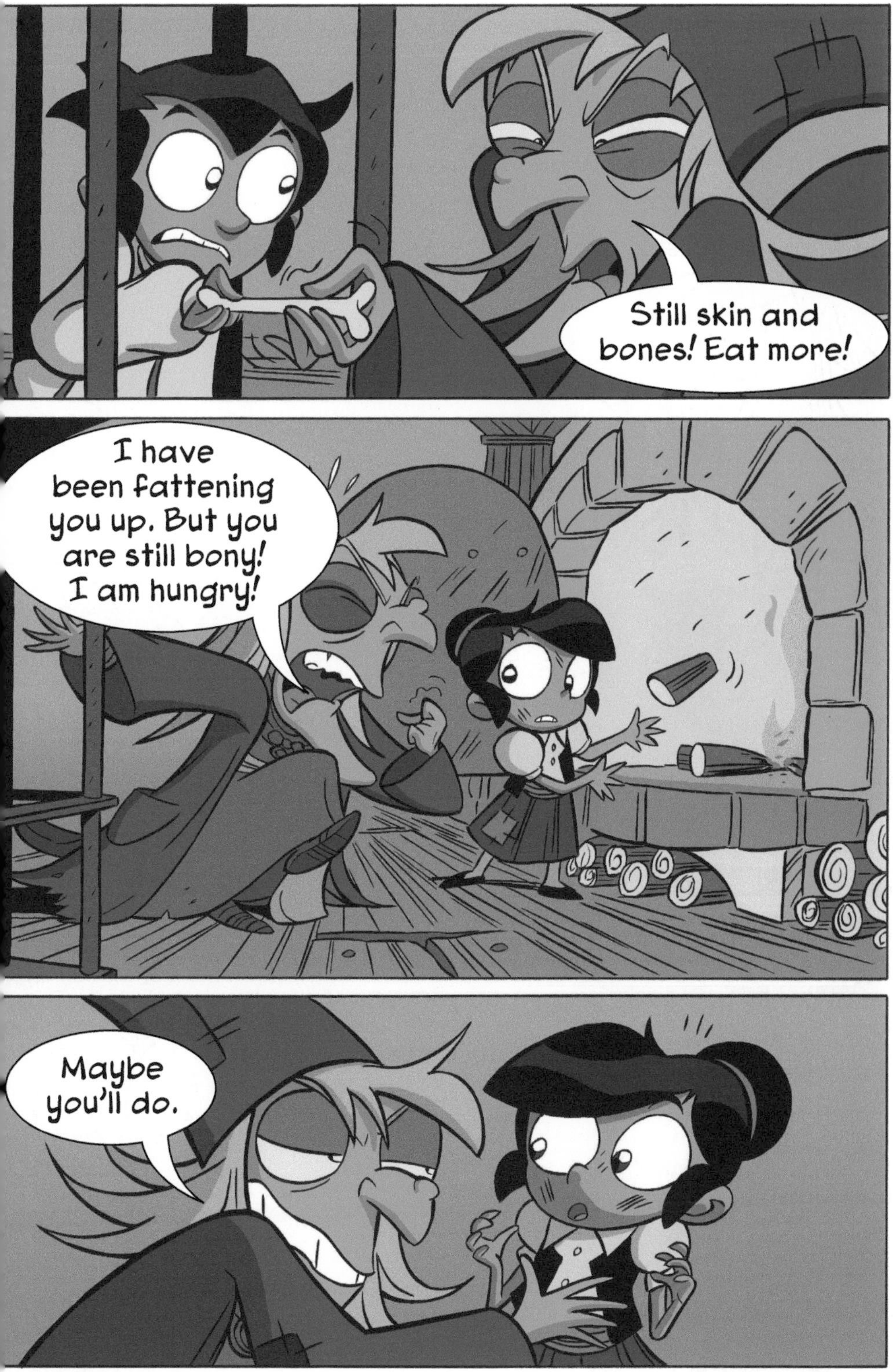
Still skin and bones! Eat more!
I have been fattening you up. But you are still bony! I am hungry!
Maybe you'll do.

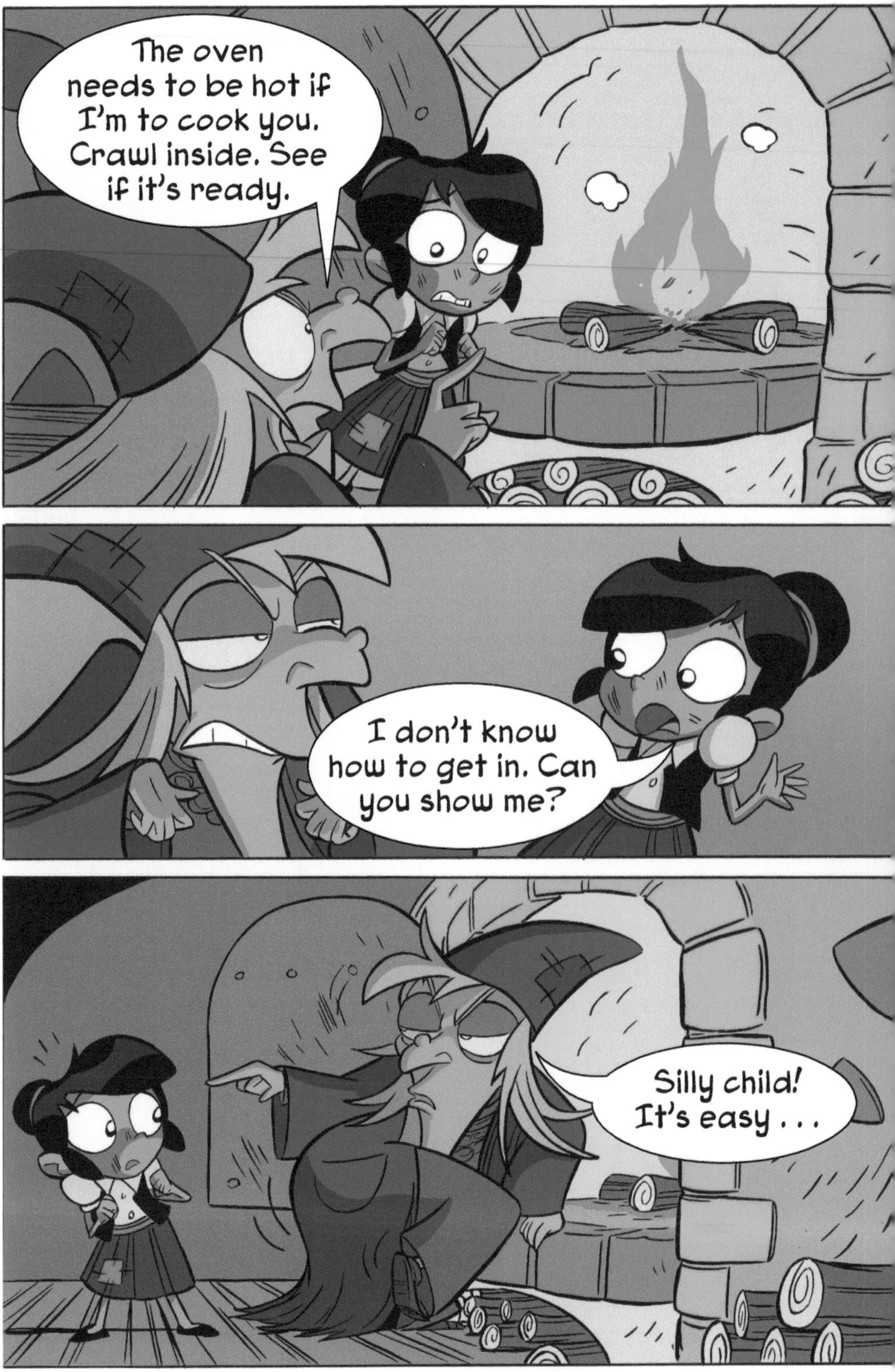
The oven needs to be hot if I'm to cook you. Crawl inside. See if it's ready.
I don't know how to get in. Can you show me?
Silly child! It's easy . . .

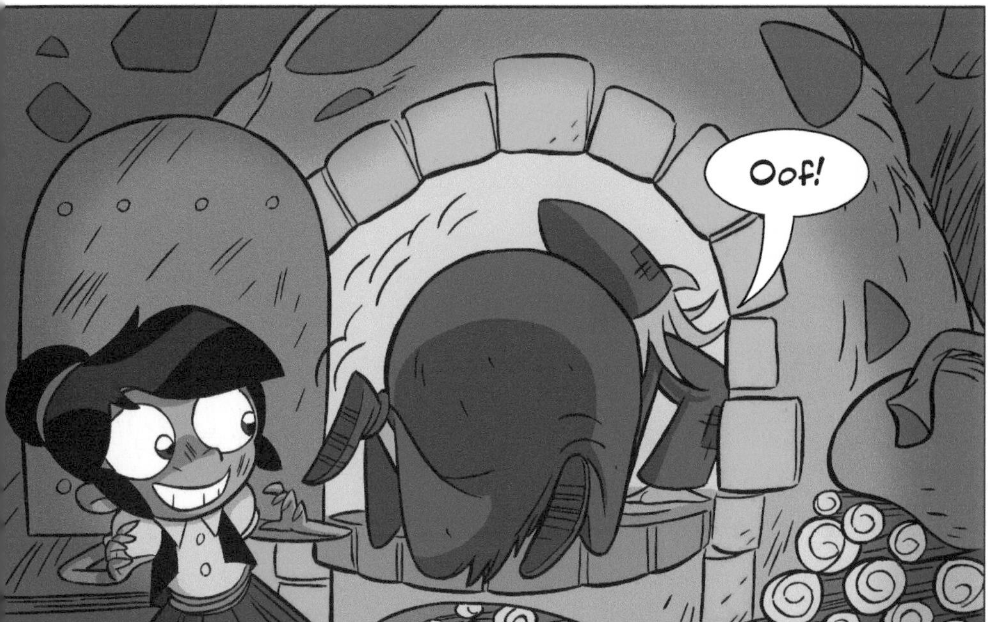
Oof!

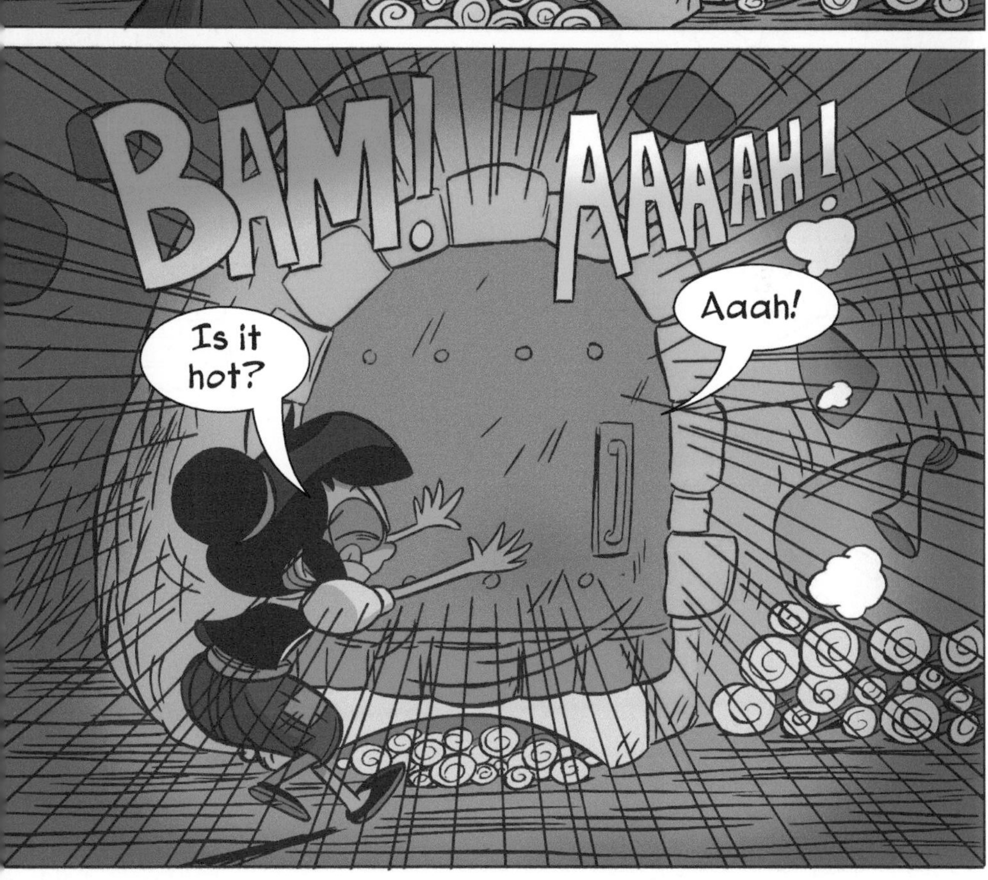
BAM!
AAAAH!
Is it hot?
Aaah!

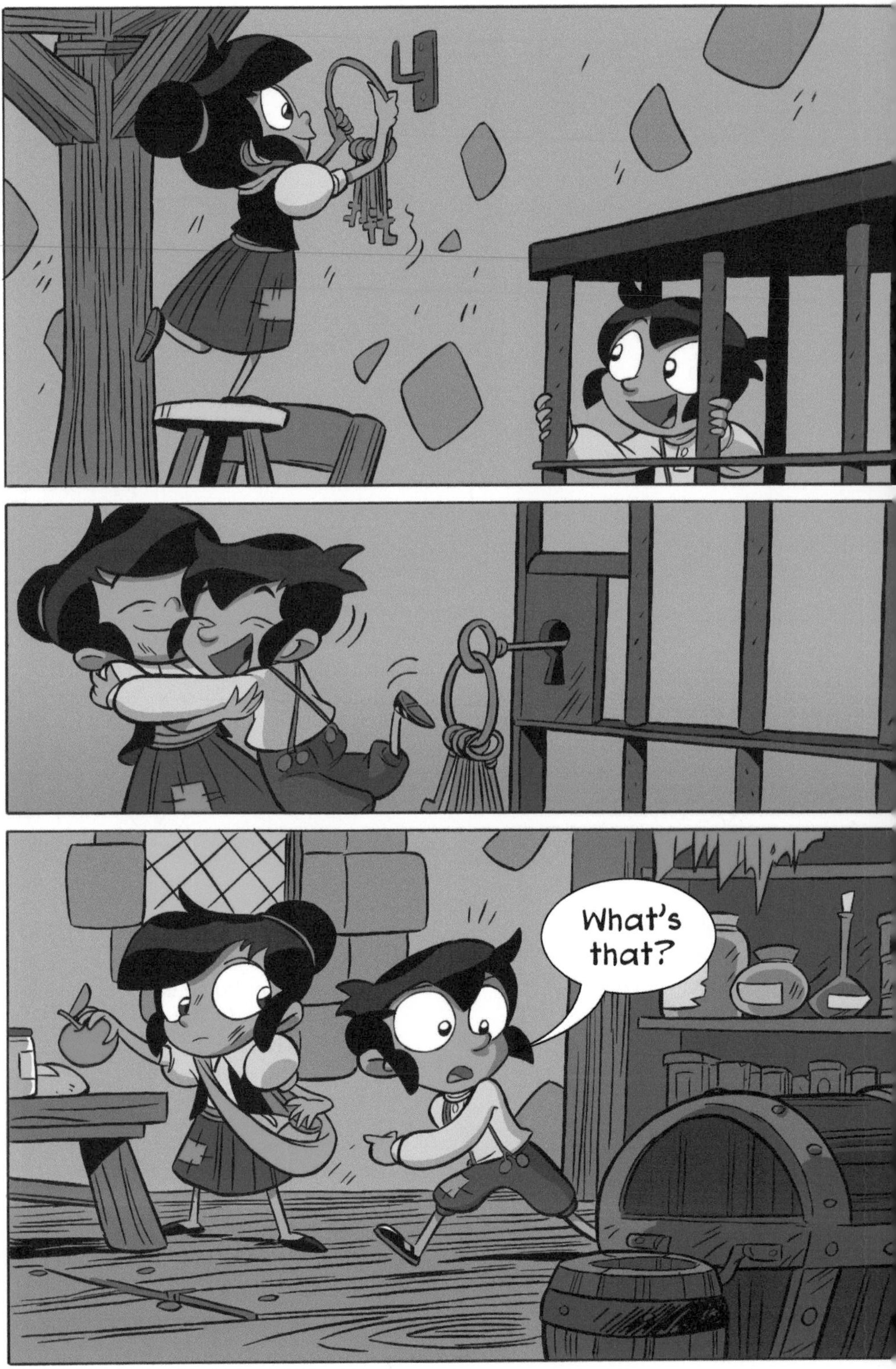
What's
that?

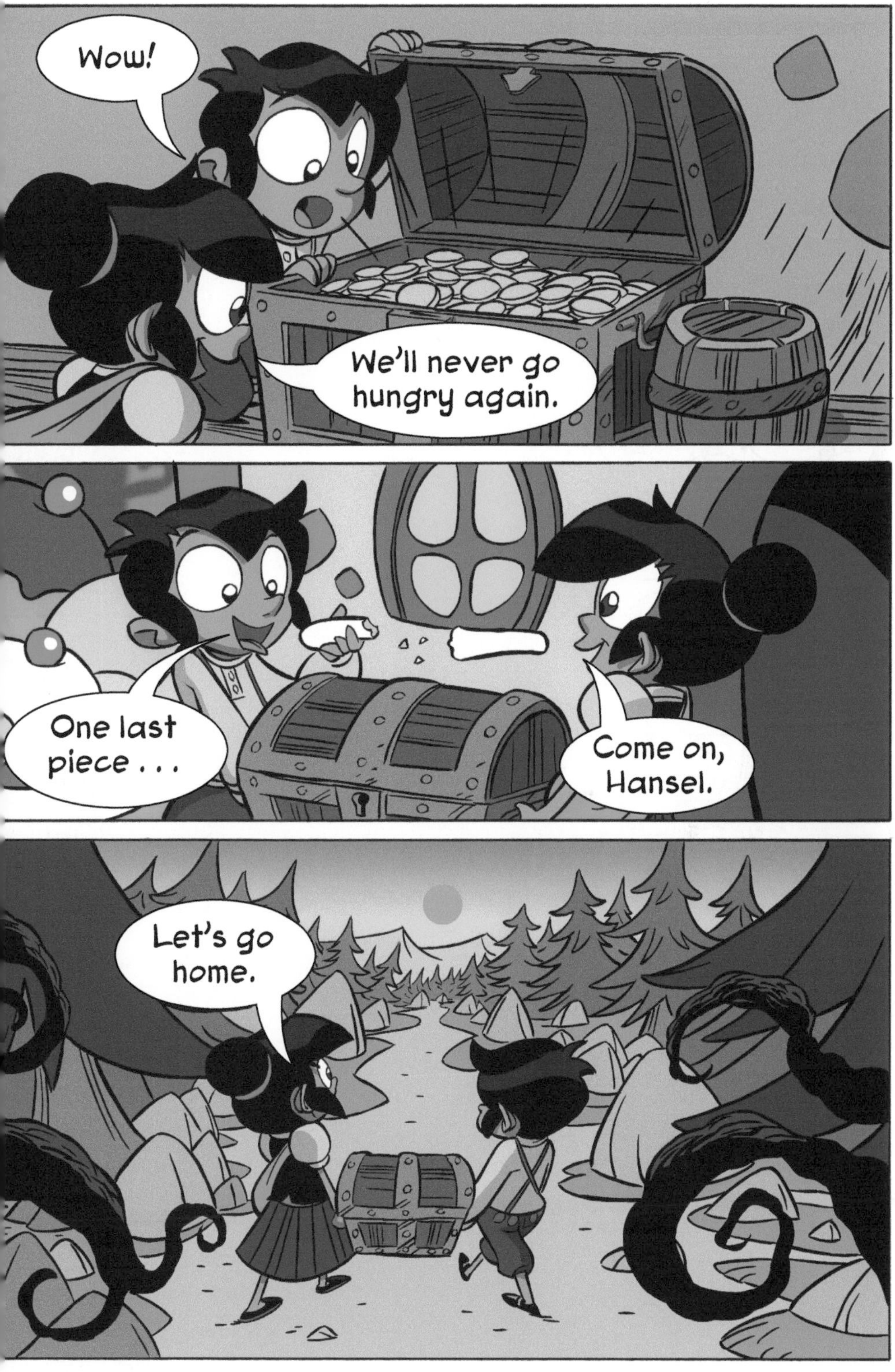
Wow!
We'll never go hungry again.
One last piece . . .
Come on, Hansel.
Let's go home.

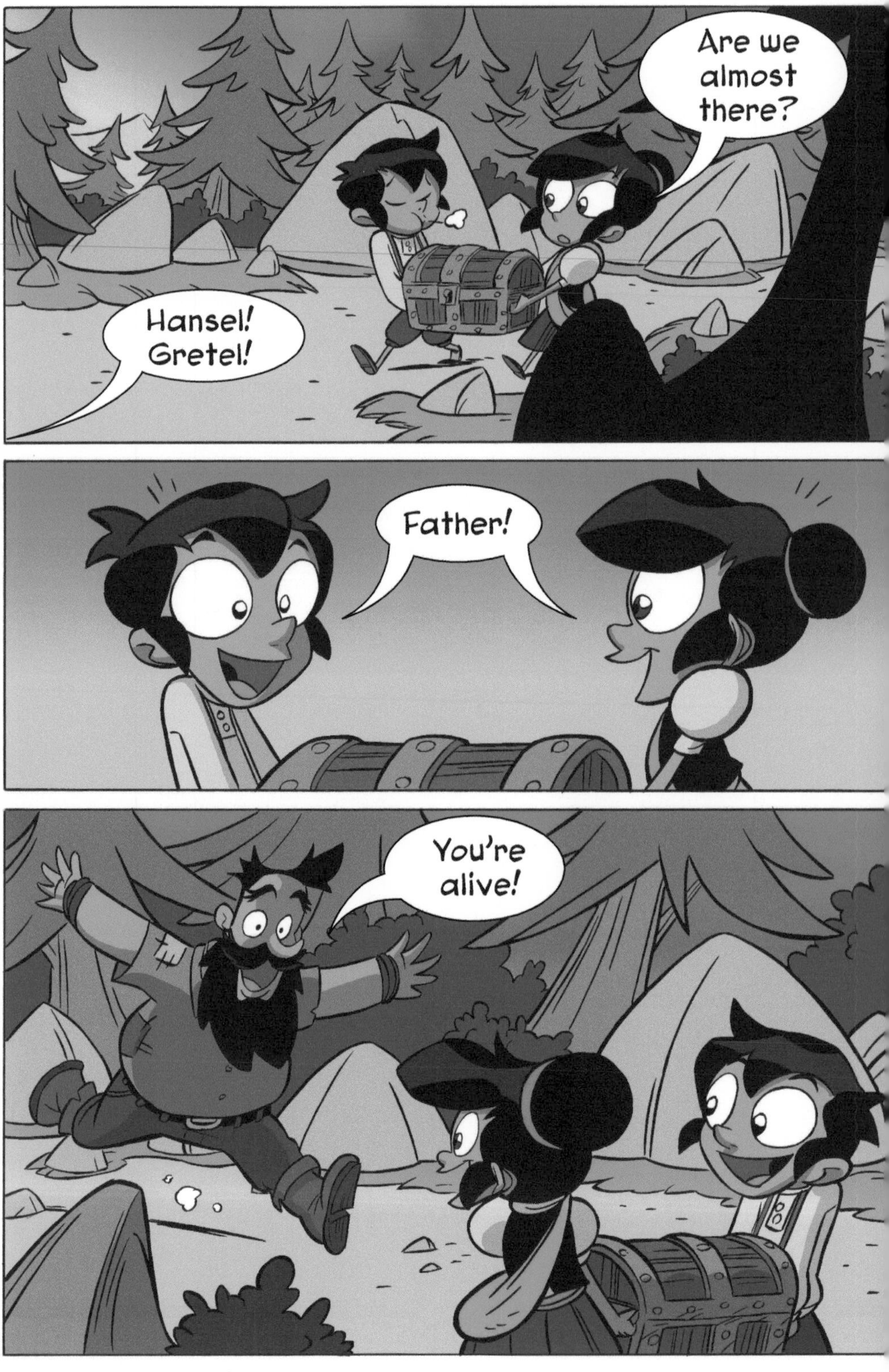
Are we almost there?
Hansel! Gretel!
Father!
You're alive!

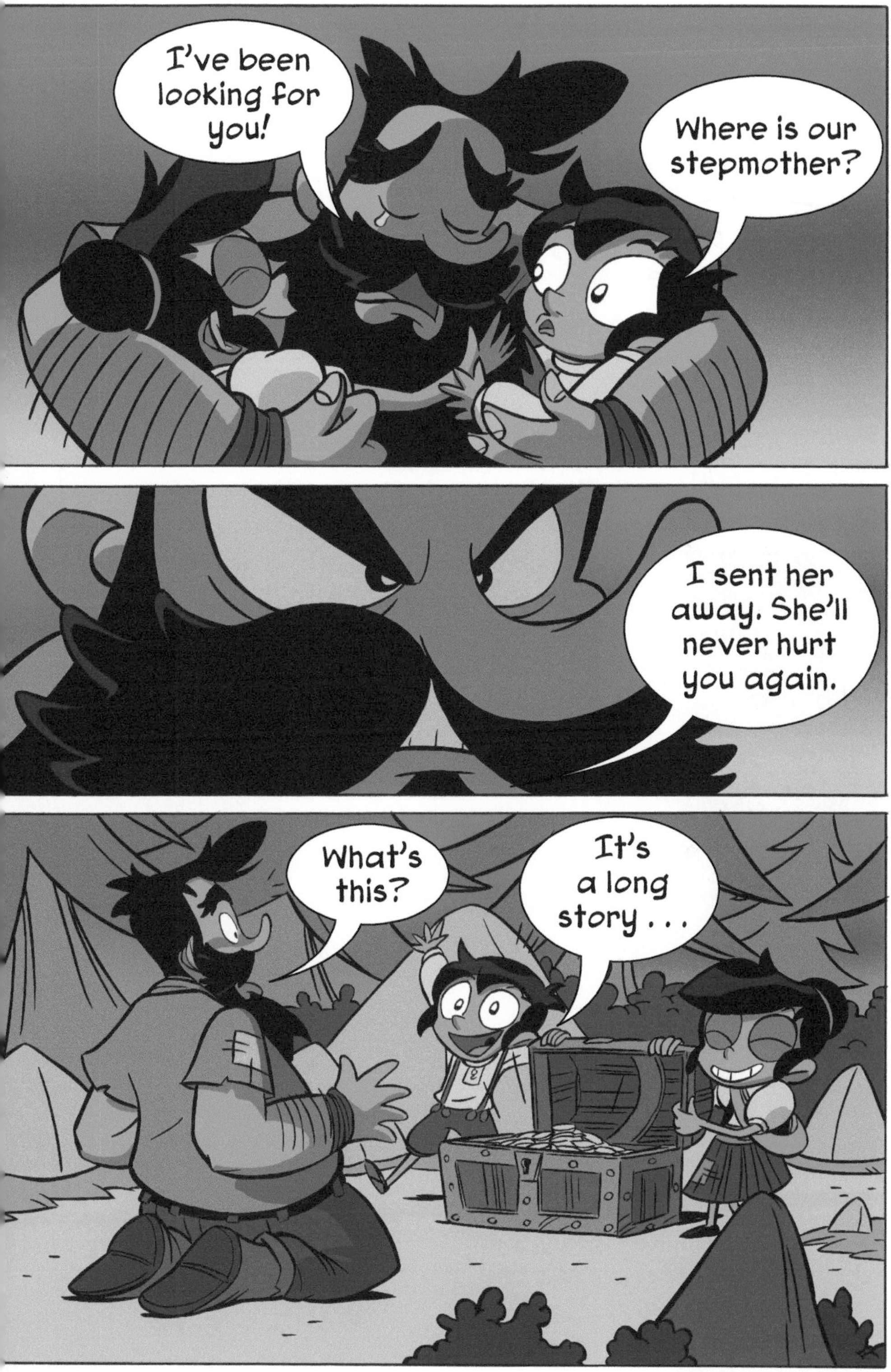
I've been looking for you!
Where is our stepmother?
I sent her away. She'll never hurt you again.
What's this?
It's a long story . . .

WRITING PROMPTS

1. Why is food so important to the story? List three reasons to support your ideas.

2. Rewrite the story from another character's point of view. Would the father, stepmother, or witch have a different version of what happened?

3. Write a story that takes place after the main tale. Should Hansel and Gretel go back to living with their father? How might the treasure change their lives?

DISCUSSION QUESTIONS

1. Why does the stepmother want to leave the children in the woods? Why do you think the father agrees?

2. Do you think the stepmother knows how the children found their way home? Why or why not?

3. Have you ever been in a situation where you felt lost, like Hansel and Gretel? How did you handle it? What did you do?

EDIBLE HOUSE

Skittle the Witch lived in a gingerbread house trimmed with candy. What do you think it looked like? Build your own and show it off.

WHAT YOU NEED:

- icing (see recipe)
- zip-top bag
- scissors
- 12-inch (30.5-centimeter) square piece of cardboard
- aluminum foil
- graham crackers
- candy

WHAT YOU DO:

Step 1: Make icing by following the recipe below. Pour icing into the zip-top bag. Ask an adult to cut a corner off the bag.

Step 2: Cover the cardboard with a layer of foil.

Step 3: Use graham crackers and icing to build a house on top of the cardboard.

Step 4: Use the icing as glue to decorate the house with candy.

TO MAKE ICING:

- Mix 1 pound (454 grams) powdered sugar, 3 tablespoons (45 milliliters) meringue powder, and 4 to 6 tablespoons (60 to 90 mL) cold water in a bowl until smooth.

TIP:

- Cutting shapes and corners out of graham crackers is easy! Place a few crackers on a microwave-safe dish. Then cover with a damp paper towel. With an adult's help, microwave for 20 seconds or until the crackers are soft. Ask the adult to help you cut the crackers into shapes using a knife or cookie cutters.

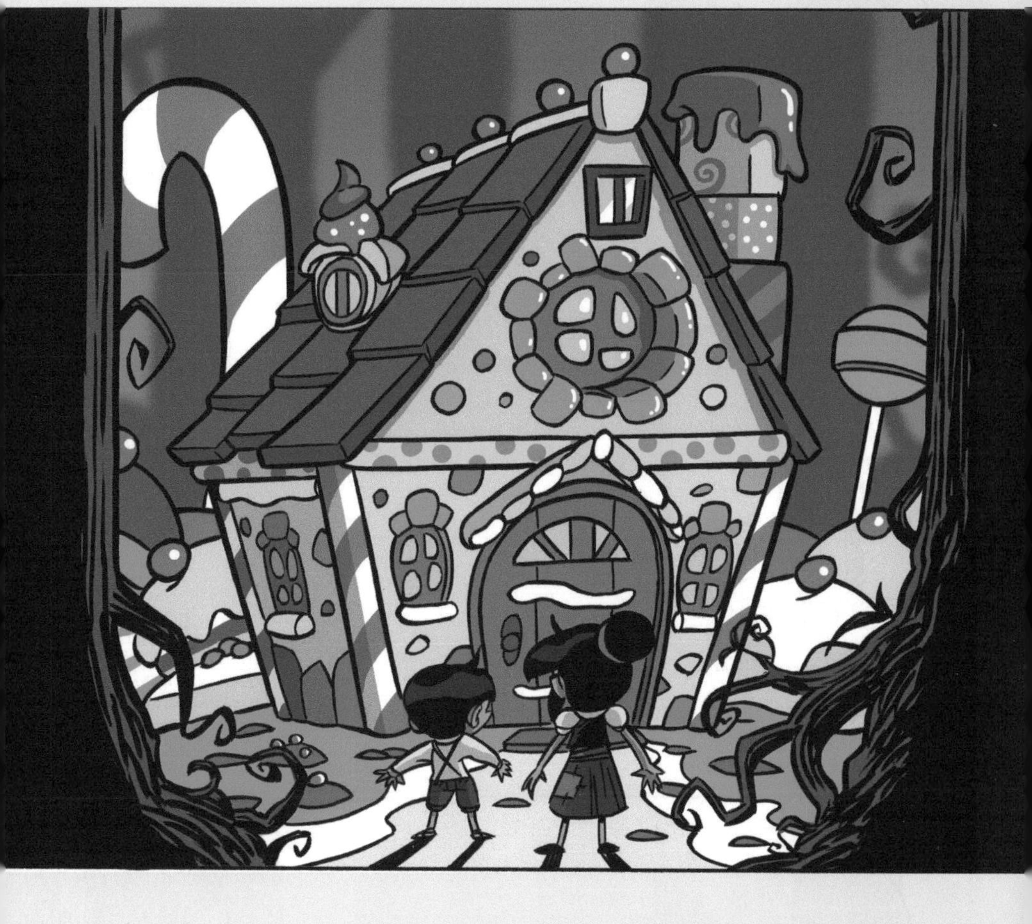

READ ALL THE AMAZING BOOKS IN THIS SERIES

CINDERELLA
DISCOVER DG GRAPHICS
WRITTEN BY JENNIFER FANDEL ILLUSTRATED BY MICHELLE SIMPSON

BEAUTY and the BEAST
DISCOVER DG GRAPHICS
WRITTEN BY JESSICA GUNDERSON ILLUSTRATED BY THAIS DAMIÃO

RAPUNZEL
DISCOVER DG GRAPHICS
WRITTEN BY JENNIFER FANDEL ILLUSTRATED BY ANUKI LOPEZ

SLEEPING BEAUTY
DISCOVER DG GRAPHICS
WRITTEN BY JESSICA GUNDERSON ILLUSTRATED BY RUSS COX

HANSEL AND GRETEL
DISCOVER DG GRAPHICS
WRITTEN BY JESSICA GUNDERSON ILLUSTRATED BY ALEX LOPEZ

DISCOVER DG GRAPHICS
RED RIDING HOOD
WRITTEN BY CRISTINA OXTRA ILLUSTRATED BY MIGUEL DIAZ RIVAS

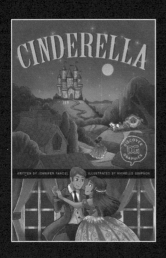